A COZY FANTASY
SHORT STORY COLLECTION

Of Becoming
1–5

ARQUIE

I0778575

Adulting is hard.
Becoming an adult seems harder at times.
You are not alone.

TRICKSY

1

One swift swipe, and my crystal was gone.

"No!" I shouted. Tools clattered off my workbench as I lunged after the gremlin.

Too late.

The naked creature stuck the green diopside into his mouth and scaled the cave wall. Even though he was only as tall as my knee, he stretched out his lanky arms and used speed to his advantage. I darted in front of the curtain of strung pebbles marking the doorway and glared up.

The gremlin paused. Hanging upside down by his chipped fingernails and gnarled toes, the nasty little thief cocked his head. His oversized eyes darted around my home.

It wasn't much, but it was my own. I'd made jewelry for weeks to scrape enough together to trade for the nest of cotton blankets and the few extra clothes. Tools and half-finished projects overflowed from the workbench carved into the wall across from my bed. A bank of solid rock lay behind the wall, so I had plenty of room to expand my cave when I needed more space.

Gremlins were a nuisance us dwarrow never seemed to be able to rid ourselves of. The creatures had pale, wrinkly skin, small torsos, and long, skinny limbs. While dwarrow made their homes in the larger caves, gremlins could slip through the cracks. The cave systems were simply too complex to fully eradicate them.

"Give it back!" I hissed at the creature. I'd worked too hard on my friend's surprise for this imp to steal it.

He spread his thin lips in a grotesque grin. The green of my crystal peeked between the gaps of his nubby teeth. His kind didn't speak, but they sure seemed to know what we meant.

I eyed a copper pot full of scrap metal. Could I trap him?

Before he could come up with his own plan, I snatched a pair of pliers off the ground and threw them at the gremlin. He scuttled back, giving me a brief window to dump out the scrap metal and heft up the pot.

Chucking another chunk of metal at him, I rushed forward. He panicked and dropped from the ceiling.

I dove.

Copper clashed against stone. The gremlin scrambled to the side.

"Gah!" I yelled, trying to scare the creature away from the door. The small shift of my body gave the gremlin enough room to skirt around my flank and sprint out of the cave.

I burst into the tunnel, but the gremlin was already gone. He could have turned left towards the other family caves or right into the depths of the mountain. Either way, he'd disappeared. I huffed in irritation.

Gremlins stole two things: trinkets and treats. Over the years, the bakers and I had mapped out a system of crevices the gremlins liked to use and the location of their nests. The tricksy pests had stolen so many crystals from me I'd memorized the map and become somewhat of an expert at retrieving my trinkets. At least as much as one could. The success rate was still quite abysmal, as my attempt with the pot proved.

In any case, I didn't have what I needed here. My family's cave wasn't far, but it was tucked deeper than most because my parents had carved extra rooms for my brother and I when we were young.

Soft yellow light illuminated the tunnels as I headed off. Besh's mother had enchanted trails of yellow apatite to glow. I smiled. My cave had a few more crystals than most. Besh gifted them to me when I finally moved out of my family's cave.

Besh and her family had fled their topside home when war broke out a decade ago. It took some convincing for the older dwarrow to accept them, but now the humans were as much a part of the clan as anyone else.

Through the years, Besh struggled with the absence of the sun more than her parents. My mother and I regularly frequented the hot spring pools together, and she suggested inviting Besh and her mother along. Something with the bioluminescent algae and minerals helped boost Besh's spirits. Besh and I grew close, with her being an only child and with me only having a brother. Now that we were grown, it was harder to make room for girl time, but we still went when we could.

"Oh, this is wonderful!" I exclaimed, pulling back the beaded stone strings and stepping inside my family's cave. "Besh is going to love this."

Shards of blue stained glass twinkled from the ceiling and cast fragments of light everywhere. Giant chalk trees covered the walls of the main room, all sorts of green and…and purple?

"Don't jinx it, Noop!" my brother said. He stood in the center of the chaos, streaks of color staining his skin. His brown hair was mussed, and bits of string were tangled in his beard.

Rew was twenty, two years younger than me, and still lived with our parents. We were both about the same height at three and a half feet, which was surprisingly tall for dwarrow, and wore similar rough-spun clothes. I liked to keep my head shaved, though, so I could decorate my scalp with bits of crystal. Although I'd been too busy today to put any on.

"Purple?" I asked. "Why are the tree trunks purple?"

"Is bark not purple?" Rew frowned.

I laughed. "It's brown."

"Even if that's true, there's no time to fix it," he huffed. "Ma said they'll be back from the pools in an hour. She won't be able to distract Besh for much longer."

Oh, no.

An hour to find my crystal? *And* finish the surprise? Worry gnawed at my insides. I'd carefully planned out the day, and my family had been more than willing to help, but it'd all fall apart if I couldn't get the crystal back in time.

"Does she have any sulfur?" I asked. "I used mine up last week."

Rew tilted his head towards the back hallway. "Should be some in the little cave," he said.

I nodded my thanks and rushed into the short hallway.

My father had carved out the little cave for my mother to store spices. Over time she'd filled it up with other supplies as well.

Finding the awful-smelling powder, I swept past my brother and out into the tunnel. Rew had already returned to drawing more purple trunks.

I marched into the adjacent tunnel, straight for the main vein of crevices the gremlins typically escaped into. Their nest was too deep to get to, but I could smoke them out. I dumped a pile of the sulfur as close to the crack as I could. Taking a flint and steel from my belt, I stuck them together until the sparks took life in the pale yellow powder.

Thankfully, Besh was far away, and her parents lived on the other side of the cave system. Sulfur fumes were toxic to humans, but dwarrow and creatures of the deep had adapted. That didn't mean gremlins were immune to the nasty smell, though.

I covered my mouth with the collar of my shirt and stepped back. The ceramic sulfur jar was now empty, and the perfect shape to trap a disoriented imp.

Only a few minutes later, a dozen wriggling bodies poured out of the network of cracks. I searched for the thief, the one with dark blue eyes, a slight bump on his head from falling from the ceiling, and stained fingers.

Oh yes, after the baker discovered the sulfur method, I'd coated my ceiling with graphite. Much, much easier to find thieves with black fingers. As if on cue, the culprit scrambled out of his hole, his eyes blurred from the gas.

I pounced.

This time, the pot went over his head. I scooped him up and slammed the lid on. The gremlin rattled around and pounded on the jar, but I held it tight.

"Oh, calm down," I tutted. "You've got nothing to worry about if you give me back my crystal."

I stamped out the sulfur with my boot and started the trek back to my cave. The other gremlins scattered, not interested in the slightest in helping one of their own.

I made my way over to the edge of my workbench where a small cage was secured to the stone. The thin bars were constructed to hold a gremlin until they cooperated. Gremlins were simple creatures, but they weren't stupid.

I took off the top of the jar, dumped the gremlin, and closed the door quickly so he couldn't escape. The gremlin wrapped his fingers around the bars and shook. When that didn't work, he tossed a nasty glare at me.

"Yeah, yeah," I said and turned towards my bed.

My blankets were arranged on a thin slab of stone that covered a cellar. I crouched and pushed the heavy slab over with a grunt. Gremlins snatched what they could find, so we made sure they couldn't find what we didn't want them to steal.

My cellar was bigger than most, since I stored both my food and jewelry below. I climbed down three notches and hopped the rest of the short distance. I grabbed a slice of dried apple, moved the slab back, and returned to the gremlin. His frantic movements calmed when he spotted the yummy treat in my hand.

I held it up. "Open," I said.

The gremlin peeled his lips back but didn't move his jaws. Thankfully, I could see the diopside still in his mouth. Sometimes they stashed trinkets before fleeing the sulfur.

I stretched out the treat, a hair beyond his reach. "Trade?"

The gremlin scowled and smooshed his lips together forcefully. I held his gaze as I took the tiniest nibble of the dried apple and overexaggerated the chewing motion. "Mmm."

The gremlin swallowed. I smiled.

"Traaade?" I offered again.

The gremlin extended his tongue and deposited a slimy green crystal into his graphite-covered palm.

He tried to swipe the apple without giving me the crystal, but I pinched the treat tight. He wasn't the first gremlin with that idea.

"Trade," I said a third time, using a much firmer tone.

The gremlin made a grumbling noise in his chest but reached his hand out. I took the crystal and gave him the apple. A sense of relief washed over me when I had Besh's present back in my possession.

He stuffed the whole slice into his face before I could blink. I sighed and unlatched the cage from the workbench. Gremlins hadn't quite figured out how to savor their treats.

I hefted the cage up and hurried through the tunnels towards the rushing spring. A swift underground river had worn away a small section of rock big enough to squeeze the cage into. I'd found it years ago, and all the gremlins I caught received the same treatment.

The gremlin squeaked and shook the bars of the cage. I didn't relent. Sinking the cage into the water, I reached down and opened it. The current swept the gremlin into the bowels of the mountain.

He'd get all turned around and choke on a little water, but the journey wouldn't kill him. Sometimes negative reinforcement correlated with a dip in robberies. I yanked the empty cage out of the water and hurried back to my cave.

Tossing it in the corner, I grabbed the rest of the supplies I needed to finish Besh's gift and worked as fast as I could. When it was done, I hopped off my seat and made for the door, but paused before I crossed the threshold.

Maybe I could…

Snatching a case of little jewels and a vial of homemade glue, I began securing them onto my scalp. I set the light aquamarines, then went in with darker sapphires, and finished with dozens of tiny blue tourmalines. Before the adhesive was set, I rushed towards the pile of clothes to change out of my stained work shirt.

I tripped over the pliers. Cursing, I threw on a new tunic and used my dirty one to clean the crystal one more time.

"Good as new." I grinned. But there was no time to waste.

I ran as fast as my little legs would take me. The yellow crystals became a blur as I raced through the tunnels. My chest was heaving by the time I arrived back at my family's cave.

"Where have you been?" Rew hissed. He frantically picked up the last of the chalk from the floor and shoved it into his pockets. "They're almost back!"

I combed a hand through his hair, trying to tame the rebellious strands. "Well, I'm here, aren't I?"

Footsteps echoed down the tunnel.

"Go!" Rew whispered, shoving us both down the hall and into the little cave.

"Now, now," Ma said outside the cave. "That'd spoil the surprise. Close your eyes, dearie."

I peeked my head around the corner. Ma led Besh through the stones and into the middle of the room.

My friend had wavy brown hair cut below her ears and brooding dark eyebrows sitting above a thin nose. Her cheekbones had become more pronounced in these last few years, but her big smile remained a constant.

"You can open them," Ma said gently.

For a moment, Besh didn't react. Then the shock wore off, and tears filled her eyes.

Even with the purple tree trunks, the forest looked real enough to me. The stained glass on the ceiling scattered stars across the stone. Rew even had time to add a few red flowers to the floor.

Rew and I jumped out and shouted, "Surprise!"

Besh started and covered her mouth with her hands. "You…you did this for me?" she asked in a small voice.

"Of course," I replied.

"No, couldn't be for you," Rew teased.

"But it's not my birthday," she protested. "And the festival isn't for another few months."

I wrapped her in a big hug and rested my cheek on her stomach. "Friends don't need a reason to love each other. I know you've been missing home, so we tried to bring home to you."

"Tha—" Besh gasped. "What's on your head?"

I stepped back and gave her a slow twirl. "Do you like it? Your mother told me you used to travel to an ocean. She said lots and lots of blue. Does it look like an ocean?"

"Sure." Besh giggled. "You've definitely got the blue covered."

Ma drew the curtain of stone strings back and secured them to the sides of the doorway. More yellow light from the tunnel hit the glass and refracted across the walls.

"And the trees?" Rew piped up. He leaned in close, eager for her opinion. "Do the trees look real? Noop said tree trunks are brown, but I don't believe her. Your father told us stories with purple trees."

Besh glanced at me and smiled a wide, toothy grin at Rew. "You know he was pulling your leg, don't you?"

I laughed a deep belly laugh and hugged my center when it started cramping. "I told him!" I gloated. "I told him, and he didn't listen."

"They look wonderful, though. Truly." Besh gave my brother a light hug. "This is an amazing gift. Thank you both."

"I have one more surprise," I announced.

Besh's eyes widened. "But this is already so much!"

I took her hand and placed her gift in it. When Besh opened her fingers, her bottom lip wobbled.

Weeks ago, I'd started shaping the raw diopside into a rectangular prism with pointed edges and polishing it until it gleamed. After several conversations with Besh's mother about how it looked, I etched a willow tree into the thickest side. Hundreds of vines. Thousands of leaves.

I'd set the crystal down to work on the other necklace bits when the gremlin stole it. But now it was complete, and the willow tree pendant hung from a simple silver chain.

Besh held the necklace close, taking in the intricate details. "I used to play under the willow tree near our house," she whispered.

"I know," I said.

"I love it!" Besh threw her arms around my neck. "Thank you, thank you, thank you!"

Ma cleared her throat. "Before I leave you children be, *I* have one more surprise."

"What?" I exclaimed.

Ma winked and disappeared into the hallway. She rummaged around in one of the rooms and came back with something behind her back.

"Any good celebration needs a little treat," she said. She brought her arm around to reveal a plate of golden pastries sprinkled with cinnamon.

"Cookies!" Rew shouted. He rushed forward and snatched two off the plate. Jogging back, he offered one to Besh. She grabbed it and took a big bite.

My friend's wide smile returned, and happy tears trailed down her face.

FLOURISH
2

Pack, load, strap, repeat.

Pack.

Load.

Strap.

Repeat.

If I kept moving, maybe the tears wouldn't fall. Maybe I could make it through without breaking apart. Maybe…

The small bundle fell off the saddle and scattered my clothes on the stable floor. I rested my forehead on my pony's shoulder and let out a sob.

Gippy, my dappled gray darling, lifted her head and gave me an encouraging whinny.

I sniffed and wiped the wetness off my cheeks. She was right. It was okay. Or at least it would be.

When I dreamed of becoming an illusionist, I didn't think moving away from home would be this hard. Our small village only had one tavern, and they preferred Ol' Benny's lute to my simple illusion spells.

I bent to pick up my clothes. Renewed determination shored up my fragile emotions. I'd find an entertainment house in the Trident. I'd learn. I'd get better.

I tied the bundle on the rear of the saddle and made sure the straps were tighter this time. Exhaling a deep breath, I rubbed Gippy's neck. She shifted her weight and stomped her leg with impatience.

"I know," I soothed. "I'm almost ready."

Bright sunlight greeted me when I left the stable. Father had built our family home on the edge of town, close enough to the tailor shop Mother could still walk to work. He'd helped me put up the small stable for Gippy a couple years ago when I'd made enough money from sewing during the busy season to purchase her.

I walked the short distance and climbed the steps. Our home was a two-story gabled log cabin with a wraparound porch. I sped through the kitchen so Mother and Nana couldn't talk to me and bounded up the staircase. The last bedroom on the left was mine.

Was.

Huh, it was weird to think this was a part of the past now.

I scanned the dusty bookshelf, the well-worn quilt on the small bed, and the jars of dried plants on the windowsill. Picking up the jar of blue denuce mushrooms, I smiled and pressed a farewell kiss on the cool glass.

I'd only found three in all my nineteen years, even with spending most of my free time exploring the forest. Denuce mushrooms had curvy blue caps and black gills. Only blooming after rainstorms, they gave me hope good things came after hard times.

Setting the jar back down, I looked over my room one final time. I didn't want to burden Gippy too much, so I'd packed a few changes of clothes, a sketchbook full of plants, my hair supplies, and a pouch of coins with all my savings.

I straightened my shoulders and went downstairs. I'd said goodbye to my brothers and Father last night since they were already out working today. Mother and Nana's parting would be harder.

Almost there, I told myself.

"Krim, did you grab your wool socks?" Mother called from the kitchen. "You know winter gets cold on the mountain."

I sighed and rounded the corner. Mother and Nana sat at the table working on a colorful quilt. Their needles wove into the fabric with practiced grace.

I'd gotten my black hair from Nana, though hers was streaked with gray. Mother's deep brown hair was still hidden underneath her cream sleeping bonnet. My eyes were hazel like Father's, and I'd gotten my dark skin and wide nose from the women in front of me. In preparation for traveling, I'd styled my thick curly hair into ten braided rows.

"I don't have room to take everything," I replied. "And winter's two seasons away. I can use my wages to buy what I need."

"Working at an entertainment house?" Nana raised an eyebrow.

Mother frowned. "I thought you were going to find a tailor?"

They meant well. I knew they did. But right now it didn't feel like it.

I plastered on a smile and squeezed all the muscles in my face so none of them would tremble. "I can find a tailor to work for until I can support myself as an illusionist."

"All those hours. How are you going to take care of Gippy?" Mother asked.

"And the Trident's a big city," Nana added. "It's not safe to be out at night."

Tears stung my eyes. I popped my fingers to distract myself. "I'll be alright. I'll make time for Gippy between shifts, and I'll be careful at night."

"Do you know who your roommates are?" Mother fretted. "What if you don't like them?"

I bent down to give Nana a kiss on the cheek and rushed Mother's hug. They wanted to calm their fears while I had to make it seem like I had none. I didn't have it all figured out. I was scared of everything they were and more, but I knew in my heart I could do this.

"I have to feed Gippy before I leave," I lied. "I love you, and I'll try to write when I can."

"Yes, please write." Nana smiled.

Mother set her needle down and rose to give me a proper hug. "Be careful," she whispered into my ear.

My throat was too tight for a response. I nodded and broke away. Giving them one last wave, I strode out of the house.

Gippy jerked her head away from the saddle as I entered the stable.

I laughed, already feeling better. "Looking for the treats already?"

Gippy turned her head and cast her eyes upwards. I untied the lead and guided her out of the stable. Swinging up into the saddle, I gave my childhood home one last look before tapping my heels into my pony's haunches.

Gippy was delighted to be out in the sun and set a brisk pace. Soon the town was far behind us.

I'd visited the Trident a few times in the past months under the guise of making supply runs for fabric, but I'd always taken careful notes of important features. I'd lined up a room, a stable for Gippy, and had a few entertainment houses in mind to look for a job.

It took a long day of riding to reach the city. I would have preferred to enter when it was light, but I wanted to get Gippy settled in with food and fresh bedding rather than wait for to-morrow.

The Trident was a bustling city, even after sundown. Music and yellow light burst from overflowing taverns. Groups of friends laughed in the streets. Lovers danced by a fountain.

But there was another side to the city, too.

Beggars slumped over where the torchlight didn't touch. Drunk patrons yelled into the air and stumbled over uneven cobblestone. Crew members stood in the shadows, watching over their territory.

I shivered and urged Gippy on. The crews were dangerous. I didn't need to get mixed up with their lot.

Retracing the route from memory, it wasn't long before we stopped in front of a quaint three-story inn. The thatched roof needed repairs, and moss grew between the worn brick. *Ollie's,* the sign read.

I slid off the saddle and knocked on the door.

No one answered.

I chewed my lip and rechecked the sign. Was this the wrong spot? Maybe he was asleep? I knocked again, too desperate to leave.

An older man with wispy white hair and oversized ears opened the door. "Hello?" He frowned. "Do I know you?"

"Mr. Ollie." I held out my hand. He didn't shake it. I cleared my throat and dropped my arm. "I'm Krim. I paid a deposit for a room last month."

"Oh, oh, yes, I remember now!" he exclaimed. He stepped back and ushered me in. "Right this way."

I hesitated. "Can I stable my pony before I head in?"

Ollie nodded. "Around back. Your room is on the top floor. First on the right."

He didn't seem inclined to give me a tour this late, but it was okay. I found the stables easily enough and bedded Gippy in no time. Arms full of my meager belongings, I trekked up the stairs and opened the door to my new home.

I wasn't able to afford something with a connected kitchen or living space, but the small room with a bed and dresser was enough. Light foot paths were worn into the floor, holes from old decorations littered the walls, and a cold breeze crept through the roof.

I wanted to collapse onto the bed and forget about my long day, but worry prickled at the back of my mind. I dumped my belongings in the corner and assessed the room. Deciding the dresser was the best option, I grabbed the edge and pushed. After much struggle, it finally slid into place in front of the door. Satisfied no one would get through without waking me, I climbed into bed and promptly fell asleep.

The next morning, I found Ollie and gave him a few of my precious coins for Gippy's hay. Once she was thoroughly enjoying her breakfast, I set off towards the first entertainment house on my list.

I had no intention of pursuing illusions on the side. I'd told my family about my more professional aspirations, but maybe it was less about appealing to their expectations and more about protecting the little spark I had.

In the daylight, the city bustled with a different sort of life. Most everyone had a package in hand or were hustling to pick one up, be it an extra loaf of bread or an armful of gowns. They were focused on their errands rather than winding down and enjoying themselves like last night.

The Trident was built into a trio of mountains, and the streets stretched up in layered tiers. I'd only been on the westernmost peak on the lowest level. All the areas probably had their own unique names and demographics, but all I knew was the richer someone was, the higher they lived. I'd have to explore once I got settled.

Even on the lowest level, the buildings were well maintained. Businesses and houses alike were mainly built from wood or a light gray stone. Hunched-over winged gargoyles overlooked the crowds below from the corners of most buildings. I snorted softly. They were quite ugly but added to the city's charm.

The bold blue and black design of Deception's Dance came into view before I could read the sign. The three-story building was crammed between a tavern and a brothel, likely a good investment for all three. Black iron molding trimmed around cerulean shingle siding. Dancing performers were molded into the details and moved in a graceful, fluid motion. They must have paid a fortune for a continuous spell so complex.

The glass double doors were tinted, but it wasn't as if I could see past the posters anyway. My feet wandered to a stop, and my eyes roamed over the faces of people I'd hopefully call friends one day.

The hand-painted posters depicted a woman and man duo act. The woman was in front with a bright blue and silver fan in front of her face. Her blonde hair fanned out behind her and blended into the flames erupting from the man's hands. He tilted his head up, blowing more fire from his mouth.

My hand hovered over the handle. What would I say?

Hi, my name is Krim. Are you hiring?

No. That sounded too desperate.

Hello, I'm Krim. I'm an illusionist and was looking to see if you had a spot open?

But I wasn't technically an illusionist yet. What if they hired me and found out I didn't have the experience?

I sucked in a breath and wrenched the door open. There was no use playing make-believe scenarios in my head.

It took my eyes a moment to adjust to the dim interior. The lobby was drenched in luxury. Wainscoting framed candle sconces around the small room. Soft orange light flickered across rich leather couches, and black velvet curtains were draped over the walls from brass fixtures.

Two sets of ropes blocked the doors on either side of the empty concierge desk set on the far wall. I picked my way through the seating and approached the desk.

"May I help you?"

I jumped. An old, short man with a topknot appeared beside me. Fine wrinkles weathered his face. He wore a simple all-black uniform with a blue silk scarf elegantly tied around his neck.

I cleared my throat and straightened my shoulders. "Hi, I'm Krim. I'm here to see if you have any illusionist openings?"

"Do you have experience?"

His face was blank. Maybe a bit annoyed or slightly intrigued. I didn't know. Did I need to be charming or serious? No well-thought-out reaction popped into my head.

"Yes," I said too quickly. "Well, actually, kind of." I clamped my mouth shut before my rambling went further.

The man shook his head. "I get a thousand of you a day. Come back when you have talent to offer."

"Well, thanks anyway," I mumbled. I ducked out the door so he couldn't see the heat flushing my cheeks. So much for professionalism.

I tried to shake off my nerves as I headed to the next entertainment house on my list. Millie's Troupe of Exceptional Illusionists was a bit different. Where Deception's Dance focused on sophisticated elegance, Millie's drew a crowd from dramatic flair and love of oddities.

My throat went dry, and the hairs along my neck rose.

Piles of burned planks and ash were all that remained of the once great home of Millie's Troupe. A few people sifted through the rubble, but most people walking by dropped their heads and averted their gazes.

"Keep moving, girl," a woman hissed under her breath. "Don't give the crews a reason to take interest."

I turned to ask what she meant, but she was already across the street. I popped my knuckles and hurried on. Had the crews burned Millie's down? Why? Illusionists were entertainers. We didn't stir trouble.

A pang of homesickness struck my chest. This would never have happened in my small village. Even when fires sometimes caught, everyone showed up to help put it out and rebuild. This? This felt like a free-for-all, and I had no one on my side but myself.

My brows furrowed. I wouldn't let myself blend into the defeated masses or scurry home to safer territory. I was going to be an illusionist. I would not give up.

I lifted my chin, and my strides were steady as I pushed on.

In the Hat looked like any other old tavern, but it was tall enough to support a balcony within. When I walked through the heavy wooden door, a perfume of stale ale clouded around me.

The entertainment house had a cobblestone stage against the far wall with dark maroon curtains behind. Rows of rickety old seats were set in a semicircle in front of it. A small bar was nestled in the corner next to a flight of stairs I assumed led to the balcony.

This early in the morning, I wasn't surprised no one was at the bar. In fact, the only person here was a man in his thirties polishing glasses.

"Show's not until dusk," he said. The curls at the ends of his dark mustache twitched when he talked.

I tugged my lips into a smile, wiped my sweaty palms, and stepped forward. "I'm actually here to see if you've got a spot for an illusionist."

The man shook his head. "Sorry, we're full for the night."

"It doesn't have to be tonight," I rushed out. My confidence crumbled. "You know, it doesn't even have to be a real spot. I'll do anything. I can tailor the costumes, help out with the bar, anything you need."

So much for not tailoring, but I couldn't help it. If I didn't get a spot here, I'd have to putt around the taverns. Battling bards and musicians for the same slots would make it harder to earn a living. I could try the central mountain peak, or farther up this one, but the commute would drain me.

The man seemed to mull it over. "You free tonight?"

"Yes!" A faint flicker of hope swelled in my chest.

"Be here two hours before dusk. You're on cleaning duty."

"Thank you!" I said, but he'd already turned back to his glasses.

I hurried home, eager to get settled and start my new life. The day seemed to stretch on. The more excited I got, the slower the sun moved. I put away all my belongings. Brushed Gippy twice. Ran to the market to grab a pastry for me and an apple for Gippy. Tried on all my outfits until landing on a deep brown tunic with gold stitching.

Finally, it was appropriate to head to my new job.

This time when I entered, several people milled about the room, and a few more sat at the bar. The man with the curly mustache waved me over.

"Here you go." He gave me a rag and a bucket of soapy water. "All the chairs need a good wiping."

"Steward!" a woman called out. She strode across the room, her red dress flowing around her. Long black hair framed an oval face and complemented her amber skin. "You haven't introduced me," she accused.

Steward shrugged.

The woman's tapered eyes narrowed. "Do you even know her name?"

When he didn't reply, I stuck my hand out, very conscious of how it ended the last time. "I'm Krim. I'm helping out tonight, but I'm hoping to have an illusionist spot soon."

"Stage name is Rabs. Very lovely to meet you." The woman shook my hand quickly, then turned a playful glare on Steward. "You didn't tell me we had a backup!"

"She's not a backup," Steward protested.

Rabs didn't pay him any mind. Instead, she took the rag out of my hand and tossed it onto the bar. Slinging an arm around my shoulders, she leaned her head in close and steered me towards the stage.

"Our opener has fallen ill," she said. "We've got to get you cleaned up and prepped!"

I swallowed. "Now? *Tonight?*"

Rabs spun me around and grabbed my shoulders. "Do you not want to?"

"It's not that!" I assured her. "I…I haven't performed all that much."

In a blink, Rabs disappeared and turned into a white rabbit. She ran around my ankles twice before shifting back. Her red dress wasn't even out of place. I remembered to close my mouth.

"My shifter form is a rabbit. A rabbit." She peered into my eyes. "It's not what you can do; it's how you present yourself. Show me your trick."

I bit my lip. *Okay, Krim, you can do this.*

Shaking out my hands, I searched for a spark of warmth in my chest. Once I did, I held on until it flickered into a steady flame. Replaying the memory in my head, I directed the warmth through my hands to form a sphere of white whisps and shaped it into a rabbit.

I wished I could add color, but that was a skill I hadn't quite mastered yet. The rabbit came to life between my palms. I directed the illusion to race around my ankles like Rabs had.

Rabs clapped her hands in glee. "Ooh, yes! Very nice. A lot to learn, but I see potential. You're going to have to find your own act, though. Rabbits are my thing."

I grinned and released the spell. The rabbit dissipated. "I can do that."

Rabs took my wrist and pulled me onto the stage and behind the curtains. "What's your stage name?" she asked as she led me to the dressing room.

"Uh…"

Rabs sat me in front of a mirror. Enhancing products and dripping candles dotted the counter in front of me. Racks of colorful costumes lined the back of the room.

"If you don't have one, we'll find it." Rabs tapped her finger on her lips. "Is this your natural hair?"

I popped my fingers. "Yeah. It's super curly, so I keep it braided."

"I see." A slow smile crept onto her face. "Do you trust me?"

My heart raced. I came for new experiences, right?

"Sure," I said slowly.

Before I'd even finished, Rabs grabbed a comb from the counter and began undoing my braids. When that was done, she coated several sections of my hair in different powders.

An hour later, I stood in front of a full-length mirror. She'd dressed me in all-black attire with an ochre bowtie. My curly hair poofed out in a bubble around my head. The powders she'd used turned parts of my hair light brown, deep orange, and white. Only temporarily, she'd assured me.

"Your hair is amazing." Rabs fluffed it to frame my face better. "Why don't you wear it like this more often?"

I bit my lip. "Sometimes it takes up too much space."

"My darling." Rabs tilted my chin up until our eyes met in the mirror. "Don't ever be afraid to take up space."

I smiled and straightened my bowtie. My heart swelled.

Rabs stepped back and assessed her work. "Now for a stage name," she said.

"Oh, I've got one now." I laughed. Rabs's eyes lit up when I told her.

"Yes! That's the one!" she exclaimed.

While we waited for the show to start, Rabs had me run through my new act and gave me a few pointers. More performers trickled in to get ready. Rabs introduced me to each one. By the time Steward came to line us up, I felt at ease.

I stood in the wings while Rabs welcomed the crowd. She looked like she owned the stage. I straightened my back and tried to mimic her facial expressions.

"And now…" Rabs paused for effect. "I'd like to introduce our very own…Calico!"

I strode onto the stage with confidence, even though my stomach fluttered. I waved to the crowd and blew them a kiss. A small clap greeted me.

That was okay. I'd earn a roaring applause one day.

While I entered stage right, Rabs exited stage left. The clap died down and stranded me center stage.

Taking a deep breath, I reached for my magic. I found the spark, but my nerves prevented the warmth from growing. An awkward silence filled the room. I furrowed my brow and tried again.

Latching onto habit, magic rushed through me. I directed it into a form like before, but this time I split it in two to make a cat and a ball of string. I held out my hands in front of me and tossed the wisp of yarn above the audience.

The cat chased, batting the toy around the room. The audience shifted in their seats, eager to follow the dramatic battle. A few laughed at the silliness.

After several minutes, I let the spell fade. Bowing deeply, I skipped off stage. A modest applause sent me off, and a grin nearly split my face.

Rabs hugged me in the wings. "You did great!" she whispered in my ear.

"Thank you!" I said in a hushed voice.

Rabs pulled me into the dressing room. "We'll go get drinks after and chat, yeah?"

"Sure." I nodded.

Rabs waved to the other performers, and they left for the main act.

I took a few deep breaths to calm my jitters. Alone in the dressing room, I wandered over to a mirror and checked my bowtie. I pulled up my hands to straighten it when something caught my eye.

I turned and rushed to the corner. Gasping, I covered my mouth.

Wedged between two bricks, next to a puddle of spilt ale, exactly where it shouldn't be, a tiny denuce mushroom flourished.

Maybe, just maybe, everything would be alright.

I raised my glass of wine to take a fake sip and gave the man across from me a pacifying nod.

Not noticing my lack of enthusiasm, he rambled on. "We're planning on expanding into Remker by the end of the year. It'll double our profits and increase—"

"My apologies," I interrupted. "Perhaps we could finish this conversation another time. My assistant has a rather urgent message."

My face ached from putting on yet another pretty smile as I excused myself. The man's demeanor crumbled. Annoyance fluttered through me. Was that all it took to destroy his confidence?

I discarded my almost full glass and strode towards the huge double doors where my assistant hovered but was most certainly not waving me down.

When I'd received the invitation to the Guild Ball, I thought it'd be a chance to meet potential suitors. But while the men looked handsome in their tailored doublets and the women glimmered under the candlelight, I found their conversation lacking.

At least the venue was pretty. Wood beams from retired ships supported the vaulted ceiling, and servers offered the finest food along the sides of the hall. Tables for two filled half the room, while the second half had been cleared for dancing. String music drifted over the hum of the crowd. One could almost miss the guards posted along the walls with their dark green uniforms, but the hilts of their swords caught flickers of light.

My loose black dress swished as I wove towards my assistant. She wore a lovely plain eggshell gown with a simple leather corset.

"You're not staying?" Sarud asked.

"I've got an early morning tomorrow," I said.

"Oh, come on, Melki," Sarud chided. The strand of brown hair she always kept out of her pack braids fell in front of her green eyes. "Work can wait. You can't let the Builders Guild take over your life."

"I'm not," I said in a gentle, but firm tone. "I'll see you tomorrow. Please make sure to grab muffins for the team in the morning. You all deserve it after securing that last contract." Sweeping past, I pushed through the heavy doors and into the fresh evening air.

"You owe us more than muffins!" Sarud called after me.

I chuckled and shook my head.

The sun hovered over the sea, casting orange beams onto the restless surface. Cobbled stone turned into loose dirt the farther south I went. Craem, the small village I called home, sustained itself by building ships for the Rizar shifter pack.

Not wanting to be involved with the shady dealings of the other guilds, my only real opportunity for growth in the pack was to be Inducted into the Builders Guild. They oversaw the production of goods, infrastructure, and ships. Over the years, I'd worked my way up negotiating the contracts for routes and ship building rather than become a laborer. My dedication had made strides in bringing the Merchant and Builder Guilds closer.

Sometimes, like tonight, my competence seemed like a curse. How would I find a partner who could hold a conversation without focusing on their accomplishments or giving bland responses? That was the bare minimum. I'd ideally think them attractive as well.

Although I'd pushed Sarud's concerns away, I yearned for more to life than work. It was lonely at the top. Taking care of a team wasn't the same as taking care of a family. I didn't know about children, but I wanted someone to share my life with. Twenty-nine was wearing on me.

I sighed and slipped out of my strappy black shoes. Always black or muted colors. Never too bright. Never too out of place. Never giving anyone an opportunity to attack my person when they disliked my business.

I hung the shoes off the tips of my fingers and walked the rest of the way barefoot. Every step away from the ball, I relaxed a little more.

My cozy cabin was propped between a cluster of pine trees. A half wall of cobbled stone encircled the fluffy clover yard, and dark moss nestled in the crevices of the wooden shingles.

I opened the door, tossed my shoes aside, and went to change into something more comfortable. The main space was split into the kitchen and a small sitting area by the fire, while a single bedroom was tucked into the back.

My home was modest, an oasis I could decorate as I pleased. Bits of wood I'd carved were hung up on the walls. Most of them were abstract shapes. The few creatures I'd tried turned out lumpy and disproportionate.

My room was simple. I'd commissioned my master builder to construct a matching pine bed and dresser set I'd pushed to opposite corners. A quilt my mother sent as a gift when I'd been promoted a few years ago lay over my bed.

I pulled the dress over my head and slipped on a faded red tunic and brown pants much softer than my previous attire. Drifting over to the mirror on the dresser, I assessed the state of my braids.

All wolf shifter packs wore their hair in three braids. Two smaller braids fed the sides into a larger center braid. The Protectors Guild usually wove bones from their defeated enemies into their hair. Sometimes the other guilds decorated their braids, but I never added anything. Why would I display my affection for something when any soft spot could be pressed on in negotiations?

However, I did display the *dima* all pack members had. A little piece of silver shaped into the wolf print sigil of the Rizar Pack was melded into the skin below my right eye.

Grabbing the tail of my braid, I undid it with deft fingers. I preferred my long blonde hair down, and I looked better with it framing my round face and hooked nose.

Once the braids were undone, I twirled around the room to release the tension in my shoulders. My hair tickled my face. I laughed and collapsed onto the bed. The minutes ticked by, and I stayed on the bed enjoying the silence of my own company.

But then a restlessness stirred in my chest. An itch to do something wild.

Responsible Melki would review the snippets she'd heard tonight and make a plan to leverage them to her advantage. Responsible Melki would go over the candidates for a needed addition to the team. Responsible Melki would even stare at the ceiling and run through how to wrestle a little more coin out of the Merchants Guild for next month's shipment.

But Real Melki? Real Melki liked making odd shapes with wood because it made her giggle. Real Melki liked to walk barefoot so she could memorize different textures with her feet. Real Melki was a curious, adventurous soul locked behind layers of masks so no one could tell she was a little different.

To succeed in society, I needed to carefully curate my personality to others' expectations. Since I was little, all I'd ever wanted was to be good at something and respected as a leader in my field. Somewhere along the way, life had chipped away at me until I'd hidden all the parts of me I couldn't bear to be mocked or attacked for.

I played with the loose ends of my hair. Why waste a perfectly good night? I'd already mentally sectioned off tonight for socializing. Anyone of importance in the guilds was at the ball… I could steal a few hours to be me. Relax. Maybe have a little fun. And so what if I made a fool of myself? The crews would be gone in a few days anyway. They always cycled through.

I grinned and went in search of boots and a warm cloak. This time when I left the house, I aimed away from the central hub of the town.

Sailor's Strip sat between the esteemed houses of the townspeople and the rowdy maze of docks. All kinds of businesses made their coin entertaining the transient crews. I never strayed this way, which made it the perfect escape for tonight.

Torchlight reflected in saltwater puddles as I entered the Strip. Loud music and off-tune singing floated through the streets. I smiled and bought a big stick of roasted venison from a vendor.

Walking down the boardwalk and humming to myself, I made quick work of the delicious meat. I'd only nibbled a few small bites at the ball so as not to appear too ravenous. I hadn't drunk anything either, because I hadn't felt comfortable letting my guard down. Had I made a social error in a blissful haze, it would no doubt be used to tip the favor of a contract against me. Secrets rarely stayed hidden with the Merchants Guild.

It wasn't that I liked putting on an act, but if I wasn't doing what I was, I didn't know what'd I'd do. I'd done everything my family and friends expected me to do to be successful. So why did I feel so empty?

A woman giggled and pulled a man out of a tavern. I stepped out of the way and bumped into a group of sailors entering.

"Oh, I'm—" I whirled around, trying to apologize, but found the group already through the door. I tilted my head to see the sign.

Third Wind.

A sly grin claimed my face, and I followed the sailors.

I hadn't played picket in years, but my master builder said this was the best place to play. I hoped I could watch a tournament. Wait…if I wasn't too late, maybe I could join! The spark of competition lit my blood.

Third Wind attracted a boisterous bunch. Three of the four walls of the tavern were built into a bar top. Candles set in retired anchor chandeliers lit the hazy room. Creaky chairs and square tables crowded the remaining space. Almost all of the patrons were singing along to a sea shanty led by a boy in his mid-teens with unruly black hair.

My confidence dwindled at the crowd, but I pushed through to the bar anyway. I flipped a coin onto the worn wood, and a breathless barmaid sloshed an ale my way.

"Lissen up, you scummy lot!" The boy hopped onto a table in the center and raised his tankard. "The Gulloway boys are here, and we don't disappoint guests, do we?"

"Ay, ay, ay-ooooh," the crowd howled. The group of sailors I'd run into shouted. Their words were lost in the noise.

"Thas what I thought!" the boy bellowed back. "Now les show 'em how to play cards. Five coppers to the bar for entry. Winner takes all!"

The boy drained his drink, and everyone tipped back their tankards in unison. Following suit, I took a giant gulp of bitter ale. I wanted to be more drunk for this—it was more fun.

People pressed into me, eager to show up the crew. I dug out a few coins from my pocket and shouldered my way back to the front. I didn't know this crew, which only added to the fun. My hopes of winning after not playing for so many years were next to none, but I didn't care. Tonight was about the experience.

The barmaid took my coins and marked the back of my hand with a black stamp depicting an anchor. The boy shouted instructions, organizing the players into fours. Two sailors and two Rizar were seated at each table.

An older woman with a tight dress and painted lips sat across from me. She seemed more interested in flirting with the muscular sailor to my right. He had cropped brown hair he kept running sea-worn hands through and a neatly trimmed beard.

The middle-aged man with gray grizzle and a pot belly to my left sorted through a deck of cards to make sure they were all there. Both Gulloways wore loose white sailor shirts and black pants. The younger man rolled up his sleeves to show off his toned forearms.

A sense of apprehension settled low in my gut. I took a small sip of ale, feigning nonchalance, but never taking my attention off the cards. I didn't want to give any of my competitors an opportunity to cheat.

"Alrighty, folks," the boy hollered. "House rules for this tourney are simple. Doubles, sandwiches, and stealing. When you're out, you're out. Winners advance until there's one left. Good luck, and let's show the Gulloway boys what we've got!"

The crowd roared. Bystanders spewed competitive slurs. I turned my attention back to my table, where the older man now shuffled the cards.

Picket was simple. An even number of people were dealt cards from a deck until there were no more. Going one at a time, each player put a card face-up in the middle. If there were doubles or one card sandwiched between two of the same number, anyone could slap the pile and claim it for themselves. The goal was to get the whole deck. If a player ran out of cards, they could steal and get back in.

The grizzled man began dealing.

I cleared my throat. "I believe you missed a cut."

"Gotta watch out for this one, Trule." The brown-haired sailor on my right laughed and kicked his mate under the table.

"That's not going to work this time, Farin," Trule said, narrowing his eyes and gathering up the cards again.

Shouts from other tables rang out. I adjusted my ale so it wouldn't get in the way. After I cut the deck and Trule dealt, the woman flipped a card in the center.

Seven.

Farin placed a two.

I put a jack.

Trule had a two.

SLAP!

Farin sniped the cards and added them to his pile. Giving me a smirk, he tossed a queen onto the table.

I scowled. Mine was an ace.

King. Three. Eight. Jack. Four. Five. Nine. King. Eight. Eig—

SLAP!

Trule snagged the stash. I kept my face even, but my fingers twitched. The woman was no help. I'd have to carry Craem's reputation on my own. We went around a few more times. My cards dwindled. When a pair of aces came along, I shot my hand out.

Too late. Trule's nails sliced into my finger. Blood welled. He grinned and took the cards.

After a couple more circles, both the woman and I were out of cards. The woman sat back and pouted, but I straightened my shoulders and watched the fast exchange of cards with rapt attention.

The blood on my finger had barely dried when I thrust my hand forward again. It was only three cards, but I was back in the game. Something in my chest shifted. The anxiety rolled into a rhythm.

I lost all my cards immediately, but the sailors both had even stacks, so I didn't lose hope. When a five slid between two kings, I slapped. This time my fingernails did damage to Farin's palm.

He narrowed his eyes. I fluttered my eyelashes with an air of innocence. It was only my human nails. They couldn't do much harm.

Because of our late start cutting the deck, the other tables finished before us. Defeated players gathered around our table and shouted at us. The rush of blood in my ears drowned out their words.

Trule ran out of cards. He threw his hands up and stood to drain his tankard. He bumped the table in the process, causing me to miss the next double.

"Back it up!" I shouted and threw down another card.

When he chuckled and didn't move, I stood and checked him with my hip. My fellow Craemers hollered in support. With a laugh, Trule retreated into the crowd. I grinned in satisfaction, but it faded as my concentration focused. Farin's lips quirked with a challenge.

I stayed standing, throwing cards faster and faster. Farin kept up the pace. His brown eyes challenged my stormy gray ones.

Throw, throw, slap, throw, throw, throw, throw, slap, throw, throw…on, and on, and on.

Sweat pooled at the small of my back. My cuticles bled. I didn't even feel it. For the first time in a very long time, pure happiness enveloped me.

Farin missed a slap. He pushed his chair back to match my stance, and I used his distraction to steal the next slap. I threw the cards faster, pushing both of our limits. Everyone else blurred away until it was only me and him.

He was down to seven cards.

Three.

Two.

Farin leaned forward and planted a hard kiss on my lips. Shocked, my rhythm stumbled, and he swiped the last slap.

"You, you—"

Farin smirked. "Are you going to play a card?"

I slammed it down with way more force than needed, determined to win. Despite his little trick, his cards still ended up in my stack.

He threw his last one down and gave a dramatic bow. Raising his tankard, he said, "Unlucky in cards—"

"Lucky in love!" the Gulloway crew finished.

I joined in the toast, gulping down most of my ale to wet my parched throat. Maybe I should be angry at the kiss, but I wasn't. Tonight was for letting loose.

The free-floating feeling of alcohol followed me to the next table, where I promptly lost to players with much more skill than I. After returning my tankard, I stepped out into the cool night air. A lute player with a small gathering sang at the corner. Drunk and happy, I twirled in the street and laughed.

"May I have this dance, my card queen?" a man asked.

I stumbled to a slow stop to find Farin's extended hand in front of me. A warm, fuzzy feeling spread through my chest. I might not have won the tournament, but I beat him, and he didn't seem to be taking it to heart.

I gave him a sly grin. "I have a better idea." Grabbing his hand, I ran down the boardwalk toward the gangplanks.

"What are y—"

I spun around and pressed a finger to his lips. "Shhh. We have to be quiet."

He grabbed my hips and pulled me to his chest. I splayed my hands on his white tunic, dizzy with the movement. Farin lowered his mouth to my ear and whispered, "Who says I want you to be quiet?"

I plunged my fingers into his short mussy hair and pulled his head back. "Gotta catch me," I murmured against his neck.

Before he could tighten his grip, I darted down the dock. My cloak billowed out behind me, letting him follow the movement. I could have shifted into my wolf form, but he was human and wouldn't have been able to keep up. And besides, I wasn't doing this to win.

Footsteps pounded behind me, and a spike of excitement pushed me faster. I wasn't familiar with the docks. Leaping over stray crates, cutting corners, and scrambling over nets, I led him deeper into the maze. I angled south since most of the ships I worked with were on the north end. Even tipsy, I knew not to potentially mess up a contract with a foolish fling.

Farin closed in. Gasping for breath, I searched for the ship with the tallest mast.

There!

Fingers grabbed my cloak. I pushed the broach over my head and sprinted towards the ship.

Farin cursed. I laughed.

When I made it to the ship, a sailor was guarding the gangplank, but no light illuminated the deck. Perfect.

I gave the guard a wide berth so as not to alert him and doubled back to the other side of the ship. Strong arms wrapped around my waist. Without giving me a chance to react, Farin whirled me around and slammed his lips to mine.

I threw my arms around his neck and kissed him back. His lips were chapped from being out at sea, but I didn't mind. In fact, the roughness stoked the warmth blooming in my core.

I giggled, breaking the tension with an air of giddy silliness. Farin rested his forehead on mine while both of us caught our breath.

"What are we doing?" he asked.

I glanced at the empty crates beside us. "Do you trust me?"

He grinned. "No, absolutely not."

I rolled my eyes. "Help me with these. I promise it'll be worth it."

Despite his initial hesitation, he insisted on lifting the heavy crates while I directed the placement. Soon they were high enough we could jump onto the deck.

"We're sneaking onto a ship?" he hissed.

My eyes sparkled with mischief. "And?"

Farin shook his head and climbed the crate staircase. Taking a moment to study the ship's rocking motion, he crouched low before launching the short distance and grabbing the railing. He hauled his body up and over.

I tried, and failed, not to watch his biceps flex with the movement. Snapping myself out of it, I left my cloak on the dock and crawled up the crates on all fours.

Farin bit his knuckles trying to stifle his snickers. I mock-glared at him and brushed my knees off when I reached the top.

Farin reached his arms out to catch me. I leapt, but my foot slipped at the last second, and my fingers grazed the railing.

I braced for the splash of cold water, but it never came.

Farin gripped my forearms, and my body thudded into the ship. We froze, our wide eyes locked onto each other. After several seconds of silence, Farin hauled me aboard.

I hugged him. "Thanks," I whispered.

"What's the plan?" he whispered back.

I winked. "Follow me."

I ran with light steps towards the center of the deck and began climbing the mast. A nippy breeze whipped my loose hair around my face. The coarse rope rubbed my palms raw, but I smiled at the pain. How long had it been since I'd done something that demanded a little sacrifice for the reward?

Farin stayed below me to catch me if I fell, but the night air cleared my head and steadied my movements. I swung into the crow's nest and helped him up.

"Look," I said, turning him to face east.

Torches lit Craem and allowed the true charm to shine. Happy crowds filled Sailor's Strip with laughter and music. Farther up the hill, families slept in their quiet homes. And even farther still, the forest blanketed the horizon.

"It's so beautiful," I said, drinking in the sight.

Farin pressed against my back and planted his hands on either side of mine. "Definitely a view to remember," he murmured.

I arched into him and hummed.

"What's your name?" he asked.

"Melki," I said absentmindedly, my attention still snared by the beauty of my home.

After a few beats, he said, "You didn't ask me mine."

I frowned. "I thought it was Farin."

"Some call me that. Others call me Captain."

My eyes widened, and I stepped out of his embrace. "C-captain?" I sputtered.

Farin leaned against the mast and crossed his arms. "You know, I've never snuck onto my own ship before."

Both of my hands slapped over my open mouth. Oh no. This was not happening.

He chuckled. "You're pretty when you blush."

I schooled my face into a scowl. It didn't hold any weight, but I tried anyway. "You could have said something. Anything. At any point."

"And miss this? I think not." Farin shook his head and clicked his tongue. "What to do… What to do…"

"I believe it is time for me to retire. Good night, Captain." I swung my leg over the basket.

Farin grabbed my wrist and tugged me back to him. "Stay," he offered.

I hesitated. He gestured to the town.

"Stay," he said again. "Enjoy the moment."

I slowly lowered my leg back down and leaned into him. He kissed the top of my head and hugged me from behind.

After a while of peaceful silence, he said, "We head out in the morning, but we'll be back in a few months. Can I expect to see you again?"

I craned my head up. "You want to see me again after beating you in cards and sneaking aboard your ship?"

Farin shrugged. "I haven't had such excitement in a long while. And besides, who wouldn't want to spend another night with a lady as lovely as you?"

I playfully swatted his arm. "That's the sailor swoon all our nanas warn us about."

"Sailor swoon?" He huffed.

I grinned.

Craem stretched out on one side, reminding me of the life I've built. The ocean stirred on the other, giving me a chance to dive into the unknown.

Steeling my nerves, I drew the captain's mouth down for a slow kiss.

Tomorrow, I had an early meeting. Tomorrow, I had to lead my team. Tomorrow, I had to put on the mask.

But tonight…

Tonight, I was free.

KINDLING

4

Mud squished under my leather boots, and a stray branch snagged my thick cloak. Grumbling to myself, I snatched it back and readjusted the bowstring across my chest to keep the fabric cocooned around me. The cold still managed to nip at my toes.

Rangers were accustomed to living in the elements, but I never turned down a chance to enjoy a warm bowl of stew. It was a rare luxury I looked forward to now that I'd reached a small village in the far reaches of Thrallen's farmland. Torches posted on a wooden arch marked the main entrance, even though a few dwindling rays of sun still lit the sky.

The buildings were simply made, but the wood looked sturdy enough. A skilled blacksmith had reinforced the doors to protect against the bitter wind and added steel decorations around the windows.

Eager to get out of the chill, I made for the Cracked Cast.

The smell of smoke and simmering meat filled my nose as I entered. My mouth watered. A few patrons milled around the room, but the tables were empty for the most part. A greedy fire burned in the hearth and licked at the charred bottom of a bubbling cauldron.

Great news: I'd found the source of the wonderful scent.

"Wynvi!" the barmaid called. "Good to see you again."

I smiled and took off my bow. Keeping a loose grip on it, I strode up to the bar. My cowl slipped, and warm air buffeted the tips of my ears. I shivered as tingles raced across my dark copper skin. My brown hair was secured into a bun atop my head with a thick strip of black fabric, which left my face and neck exposed without my cowl.

"It's been too long, Pellin," I said.

The pretty girl wore a faded brown dress and stained white apron. When she set a full tankard in front of me, the silver pins in her hair gleamed.

I reached for the ale with my right hand. The one with three fingers.

Pellin set her elbows on the rough wooden counter and leaned forward. "So, are you going to tell me about your adventures? Surely a year is enough time to get some good ones."

I took a deep drought of the dark liquid. Licking the excess from my lips, I gave her a sly smile. "Any chance I could get a bowl of that delicious stew?"

Her hand flew to her chest in mock offense. "Are you bribing me, young woman?"

I took another sip and shrugged.

Pellin rolled her eyes and went to fill a bowl while I settled at the corner table. Facing the door, of course.

She slid into the chair across from me and held my supper hostage. "Woo me with your tales of glory, oh exalted tracker," she teased.

I grinned and caved like a sand tunnel. I told her about guiding caravans through bandit-infested lands, reconnecting with an old teacher to meet his new apprentice, and helping bounty hunters track down criminals.

Pellin drank it all in. She pushed the stew towards me to keep me talking, and her eyes sparkled brighter with each passing tale.

The door slammed open, and a howl of wind nipped my face.

A thin boy, perhaps ten, heaved the heavy door shut with all his might. Red kissed the tip of his nose and ears. He readjusted his blue knit hat and jogged over to us.

"I'm so sorry, Pellin!" he rushed out. "Delfene can't make it in. The rogs broke through the fence again, and she's helping find a missing calf."

Pellin rubbed the boy's upper arms to warm them up. "That's quite alright, Mup. Tell your sister I'll cover for her. And let's hope you find that calf before the storm rolls in."

Mup's big brown eyes widened. "There's a storm on the way?"

"If my papi's old bones are to be trusted, yes." She nodded.

For the first time, Mup registered I was sitting next to Pellin.

"Oh!" he exclaimed. "The ranger's back! Maybe she could help us?"

"Don't ask me," Pellin said, gesturing in my direction.

The boy wrung his hands and ducked his head. "Um, ranger? Would you help us find our calf?"

I took the last bite of stew to savor the final dregs of warmth before we headed out.

The little boy took my pause as a rejection. "Please!" he blurted. "I don't have any money, but my family depends on our rogs. That little calf was born too early this year to make it through a late winter storm."

Pellin watched me with a guarded expression. I rarely stayed in one place for too long, and she probably wondered if I'd postpone my journey for this boy.

"How about this," she said. "I'll put your meal on the house if you help Mup."

I smiled and pushed the empty bowl towards her. Silence did wonders. "Add another bowl of stew for later, and it's a deal."

Pellin rolled her eyes. "Better get going. I can't promise I'll have any left by the time you get back."

Shaking my head, I stood and checked the quiver looped to my belt. Nine arrows should be fine if we ran into coyotes, but I'd have to make a stop at the blacksmith before I left.

"Lead the way," I told Mup.

The boy bounded to the door and used his entire body to open it. I followed with slow steps.

The sun had set while I'd been in the tavern, and the slivered moon did little to illuminate the sky. The bright torches around the village killed my night vision.

"I don't mean to rush you," Mup piped up. "But if a storm's coming, we should hurry."

I lengthened my stride but didn't change my pace. "How far is your farm?"

"Past the bend and over the hill." He pointed.

We followed the road, but I stayed to the side. There was too much mud swamping the ruts for my liking. When we turned the bend, the torchlight from the village faded. I blinked a few times to adjust my vision.

"Do you really know how to use that?" Mup waved to my bow.

"I wouldn't carry it if I didn't."

The boy swallowed and tried to hide his glance towards my hand. "Even…"

I stopped and drew the bowstring without an arrow to demonstrate. My third finger was too short to grasp the string like a normal archer, but the muscles in my other two fingers and throughout my arm had grown to make up the difference. While it had been an obstacle in other ways, my hand hadn't hindered my ability to learn how to track, which was the prized skill of a ranger.

Rangers floated through the kingdoms, taking on jobs as they saw fit. We didn't have an organized leader, per se, but we usually kept in touch by word of mouth and occasional gatherings.

I slowly released the tension and lowered the bow. "When you ride a horse, do your feet reach the stirrups?"

Mup flushed. "No."

"But you still ride," I said, pinning him with a serious stare. It wasn't a perfect example, as Mup would grow out of his predicament in a way my hand never would. However, most of the time when someone struggled on the beaten path, they could blaze their own trail just fine. "My disfigurement does not define my future. Perseverance is power."

Mup cocked his head and nibbled on his lower lip. "Were you born like that? Or were you already a full ranger before it happened?"

"Does it matter?" I asked. "I may have been born like this, but tomorrow my foot might find a bear trap, and it wouldn't make me any less a ranger. The only thing that matters is my willingness to look at other options, my determination to follow through on my intentions, and my ability to hold onto hope long after others might give up."

Mup fell quiet, silently following in my footsteps and chewing on my words. When we reached the farmhouse, a single candle lit it from within. Mup angled towards the big barn instead and sprinted ahead. By the time I'd caught up, he came out with a lantern and a coil of thin rope.

I brought my hand up to shield my eyes. "No, no. Please put that back."

"But how are we going to see?" Mup cried.

"I'll show you," I said. "Can you take me to where the rogs got out?"

Mup reluctantly hung the lantern on the side of the barn. Tucking his hands into his armpits, he trudged into an empty field.

Three main pastures were fenced off beyond the barn. Several dozen dark shapes were outlined in the gloom to the front and right of us. Rogs were large beasts with shaggy fur and a strong horn on their nose. They fared better than cows in the tough conditions. Mup's family had divided the dams and calves from the steers since they required different feed.

I kept my pace steady while Mup's picked up. Soon his figure disappeared into the shadows. I followed his tracks and kept an eye on the ground. Patches of snow dotted the wet earth, caught in the fluctuating temperatures when spring tried to take hold and winter fought back.

Hurried breaths broke the silence.

"Wynvi?" Mup called out. "Ranger? Where are you?"

I set my hand on his shoulder. "I'm here."

The boy jumped. "I thought I lost you!"

"You have to slow down," I chided. "You won't be able to find anything bumbling about like that."

A flicker of frustration furrowed his brows. "No light and now you're telling me to slow down? We don't have time! If the storm doesn't get the calf, coyotes will."

I pointed to the ground. "Do you see that?"

"Mud?"

"Yes. Look closer."

The boy squinted. "It still looks like mud."

"See the dips? There are so many they all merge together. There's no way to pick out the calf's because everyone stamped all over the tracks when they ran to the fence."

Mup's face fell. "So you can't track it?"

I picked my way closer to the fence. Snow-covered pasture lay to one side of it, and a sparse forest spread out on the other. Even with steel reinforcements, the rogs had torn down a section of the thick wooden planks. It looked like the dams had originally been in this pasture and broken out before Mup's family had rounded them back up in the spare enclosure.

"Let's find out," I said.

The ranchers must have rallied here before spreading out. A few flickers of flame bobbed nearby, and voices called out for the calf.

I turned in a slow circle, trying to distinguish hoof prints from footprints.

"This way," I said.

I held out my arm so Mup would trail behind and led him deeper into the trees. The tracks were layered, so I wasn't sure if the calf had gone this way, but it was my best lead.

We went slow, oftentimes doubling back. The rogs had spread out, and the tracks branched off too many times to follow all of them. When I'd narrowed down the herd to three or four rogs, I could finally see little prints.

"Are all the other calves accounted for?" I asked.

"Yes," Mup said.

"And the dams?"

"All back in the second pasture. This calf lost his mother, and we were trying to get another to bond, but she came back alone."

I frowned. It was unfortunate, but it was nature. Stopping between a ring of trees, I turned in a slow circle and studied the ground. Coyotes howled in the distance. Their calls were a high-pitched yipping too frantic for wolves.

Mup sucked in a breath.

"It's okay," I reassured him with a pat to my bow. "Look, there. Do you see it?"

Following my pointed finger, Mup smiled. "The small dents?"

"Very good." I smiled.

Mup beamed.

Setting off with a tingle of hope, we went deeper into the forest. The ground sloped down, water rushed below, biting wind cut through the trees, and faintly, very faintly, a calf brayed.

"Do you hear that?" Mup whispered. "It must be down there!"

I nodded and pressed a finger to my lips. Zigzagging down the hillside, the boy and I reached the rocky bottom. Mup raced the last few steps.

The shaggy brown calf brayed when he spotted us peeking over the ledge. A small cream nub of a horn sprouted from his nose, and wet fur clung to his shivering form. A rocky cliff trapped him against the racing river's edge.

"How'd he get down there?" I asking, scanning the rocky terrain.

"I may not be very old," the boy said, "but I've learned never to underestimate a wandering rog."

I chuckled and tried to put together a plan. Mup was smart to grab rope. There was a sapling wedged in the rock near the edge, but it didn't look too sturdy.

"Can we tie the rope to the tree?" Mup asked.

I walked over to it and shook the slim trunk. It felt stronger than it looked. "We'll have to make it work."

"If you go down, I'll stay up here and hoist the calf up," the boy suggested.

"It'd be better if you go down," I said. "The calf is one thing, but if anything goes wrong, I doubt you'll be able to lift me out."

Mup flushed and rubbed the back of his neck. "I'm actually afraid of heights."

I shook the tree again, judging if I should trust it. "Alright then, let's hope this little tree holds."

Mup unwound the rope, and I tied it near the roots. Coyotes sounded again, close enough to distinguish several layers of their song. There were at least six, maybe seven homing in. Not wasting any time, I grabbed the line and pushed off the ledge. Even though the rock was rough, there were only a few major protrusions.

The calf greeted me with a loud *moo* when I reached the bottom. Droplets of freezing water sprayed me and slicked the rock.

"Come here," I beckoned the calf.

The poor creature had spent all his energy shivering and didn't have any left to struggle. I looped the end of the rope around his body as best I could to support him on his way up.

"Did you make it?" Mup called out. I could barely see him at the top.

"Yes!" I replied. "Start pulling!"

The rope went taut, but the calf didn't lift. Nervousness fluttered in my stomach. Was Mup strong enough?

The rope jerked up, and the calf balked as his hooves kicked air. I lunged to steady him before he crashed into the cliffside. The calf panicked at my sudden movement and struggled against the makeshift harness.

Mup lost his grip, and the calf dropped back down. I rubbed the creature's head to soothe him.

"You can do this!" I encouraged the boy.

Mup didn't respond. Probably frustrated or embarrassed or both.

"Loop the rope around the tree and pull!" I called. If he wasn't strong enough, Mup needed to use leverage.

The calf rose a smidge. It started to struggle again, but I kept it away from the rough rock.

"That's much easier!" Mup shouted.

I smiled. He'd be able to do it if he put his mind to it.

The calf made slow progress, but inch by inch Mup pulled the braying creature up until he disappeared over the ledge. The empty rope tumbled back down.

"Got him!" Mup yelled.

I grasped the rope and started hauling myself up. My right hand didn't hinder me. In fact, it was stronger than my left from using my bow.

CRACK!

The rope went slack, and wind rushed in my ears. A funny sense of free fall flipped my stomach before I landed. The slippery rock stole my feet out from under me, and I crashed onto my tailbone.

I groaned. I was lucky I hadn't been very far up.

A sharp *snap* was my only warning before the tree smashed into the ground beside me. I flinched and covered my head out of instinct. The greedy river snatched the branches, and the current dragged it under. Before the rope could follow, I jumped forward and cut it with a dagger from my belt.

"You okay, ranger?" Mup panicked.

"I'm alright!" I picked up the frayed end of the rope and sighed. "Watch out! I'm going to shoot an arrow up."

A rope, I could climb. A slick cliffside? No.

I picked the end of the rope apart until one cord was isolated. The knot wouldn't be tight enough if I used the whole thing. Pulling an arrow out, I tied one of the cords around the thin shaft. It was easier to wedge the arrow between my knees and use the pressure to hold the little ends in place while I used my left hand to tie.

Once it was set, I slipped my bow off and nocked the arrow. The rope would throw off the aim, but thankfully I only needed it to go up.

"You ready?" I called out.

"Yes!" Mup's head popped over the ledge.

I drew back the string until my hand brushed my cheek. The muscles in my arms and back strained, but in a comfortable, practiced way.

The arrow loosed and overshot Mup. He scrambled after it.

"Got it!" He raised the rope in triumph.

"Alright, now is there anything else you can anchor it to?" I asked.

"There are some rocks up here. Let me try those!"

I waited until he called down again before testing the rope with my weight. It held, but I wanted to climb quick just in case. I slung my bow across my back and heaved myself up.

When I rolled over the ledge, Mup collapsed on the ground. I raised my eyebrows. Yes, there was a rock, but it was much too big to tie around. Mup had trailed the rope along the backside and propped his feet against it to hold the rope for me.

"Well done," I said, brushing myself off.

Mup grinned and stood on shaky legs. "Thank you."

I took off my cloak and wrapped it around Mup's trembling shoulders. The calf brayed, and Mup pulled the rope up to tie a lead around his neck.

"Let's get you both back before you freeze," I said.

Mup nodded and began walking back. The coyotes yipped again, but the danger didn't seem as dire with the calf in my care.

The wind picked up, and my thoughts turned to the heat of the tavern and Pellin's bright eyes. I smiled and quickened my pace. There was no need to find tracks when I retraced our steps.

When we made it back to the barn, Mup took the calf in while I waited by the lantern. He returned with my cloak in his arms.

Offering it to me, he said, "Thank you, ranger. We wouldn't have found him without you."

"You're welcome." I smiled and took my cloak.

"Do you…" Mup lowered his eyes and kicked at the snow. "Do you think I'd make a good ranger one day?"

"Perseverance is power," I replied. "Only you can decide if you'll be good at anything."

"But I don't know what I'm doing. How can I practice if I don't know what I need to work on?" Mup's face fell.

Leaning forward, I blew out the lantern. "Start small. Train your eyes to see in the dark. Move slow. Pay attention to the world around you."

Hope kindled in his eyes. "I can do that!"

"Look for me next year," I said. "Perhaps I can make an apprentice out of you yet."

Mup rushed forward and threw his arms around me. "I won't let you down!"

"We'll see." I laughed. Patting his shoulder in farewell, I started back toward the tavern to enjoy another warm bowl of stew.

"He'll be back tomorrow. I promise we can go then," Tils said, chopping fruit with one hand for her oldest child while her youngest rested on her hip.

I gave her a strained smile. "Of course. I'll meet you at dawn."

The baby cried. Tils sighed and looked up. Strands of sweaty hair clung to her sage-green temples. "Dawn. I promise, Venlo."

I nodded. "I'll be there."

As I left Til's hollow and headed to my own, a sense of disappointment welled in my heart. I pushed it down and kept walking.

We lived deep in the mountains where the trees grew thick enough to hollow out. Sometimes we used natural branches to navigate our city, and other routes we pathed with beautiful arched bridges. Light had a hard time fighting through so much foliage, and with night approaching, the shadows grew longer.

Wisteria flowers were planted around railings and over hollow thresholds to attract fireflies to brighten the forest.

I passed many other elves on my way. The younger ones had hair and skin the shade of bright spring green. The ones with a few centuries of experience, like Tils and I, varied in shades of more muted greens. As elves aged, our complexion faded to yellow before deepening to reds and oranges. Patterns mimicking leaves and vines framed our faces and trailed over our bodies a few shades lighter than our natural skin tones.

"What'd she say?" Huck, my partner, asked when I entered our hollow. He sat on the floor surrounded by books needed to help him transcribe the scroll in his lap.

Simple wood furniture and cabinets filled the circular room. Little pins guided delicate pothos vines around the bright oranges and reds of Huck's paintings decorating the walls. A used knife, stripped stems, and pear cores were abandoned on the kitchen island.

"Tomorrow." I sighed and stole a grape from his discarded plate.

Huck's mint-green skin looked darker in the low light, and his acorn leaf patterns shimmered slightly off-white. He wore plain brown clothes, but he took great care to decorate his pointed ears with gilded silver tips and style his matching earring stacks.

I wore a flowy tan shirt and loose purple pants to mitigate the late summer heat. My skin was a deep hunter green with a collage of ferns tracing over my body. I didn't much care for wearing jewelry and kept my hair pulled back with a simple ribbon.

"Do you think she'll make it tomorrow?" Huck asked.

"Not a chance." I let out an annoyed huff and slid to sit next to him.

"Her partner can't watch the children?"

"No, he's off on a hunting trip," I said. "But if Tils can't make it, I'll go by myself."

Huck frowned. "What happened to Opece?"

"Her grandmother is ill."

"Drear?"

"Needs to help her nephew move." I tilted my head back until it thudded on the wall. I didn't know how to process the well of emotions inside, but talking with Huck only made it feel worse. It wasn't him. It was having to voice the situation instead of it only living in my head.

"You waited all season to accommodate everyone else, and none of them are going?" A flicker of frustration marred Huck's face.

"It's fine," I assured him.

His brows furrowed. "What if the flowers have already faded? What if they've been picked clean?"

I stood up, not wanting to speak my worries into life. Bending to give him a soft kiss, I said, "There's always next season."

Huck rubbed his palm over my stomach. Round, but not showing too much yet. "There's only one first baby blanket."

I smiled. "It's not quite the end of the season. There'll be enough flowers to dye the blanket."

Huck didn't look convinced. I patted his hand before slipping up the spiral staircase carved into the wall. I bypassed the middle floor with our bed in favor of the loft.

Huck had once found a book filled with pictures of stained glass from human castles. I took inspiration from it and whittled a phoenix engulfed in flames into one side of the loft. Each feather and every lick of flame was hollowed out to let light in to dry my bundles of hanging flowers.

I picked my way through the jumble of dye making supplies towards the canvas bag on the table. Checking it yet again, I made sure I had enough bread and fruit for the journey. There was also a salve for minor wounds, two water skins, and an empty drawstring sack.

When Huck and I first met, he gifted me all sorts of colorful flowers and flora to experiment with dyes. His ventures became more intense and farther abroad in his attempts to court me.

Even after we got together, his quests didn't end. He came across an old map in a scroll he transcribed and used it to find yullis flowers. The blossoms were comprised of big petals arranged in a spherical bulb. The dark purple color was a perfect rich hue, but they only bloomed in the scorching heat of late summer.

When I began dying fabric with the flowers, other elves wanted the color. Now it was a seasonal adventure for our city to gather yullis flowers.

I'd waited for my friends to go, but now it might be too late. I looked forward to this every year and with a little one on the way, I didn't know if I'd make it next year. And to Huck's point, there might not even be any flowers left. If that was the case, maybe I could make do with the two I had left over from last year.

I gripped the edge of the table. Hanging my head, I squeezed my eyes shut and took a deep breath. I loved my friends, but sometimes our relationships felt shallow and brittle.

Drear's family was large enough her nephew would have been fine moving without her. Opece's grandmother had been ill for quite some time. A caretaker could have been arranged well in advance.

And Tils? Tils liked to use her children as an excuse, even though she always assured us her partner could take care of them. I used to be understanding and gave her a lot of grace, but after so many years of being let down, I'd come to expect her absence.

I wiped my face and straightened my shoulders. An empty pit chewed at my heart, and my mouth tasted of ashes, but I made myself move. With stiff motions, I went to our bedroom, changed, and brushed out my hair.

Huck would be up late, and I'd usually join him, but the weight of emotional exhaustion anchored me to the bed. I closed my eyes and curled up.

This is ridiculous, I thought. *I can go alone. It'll be just as fun.*

But it's not the trip, is it? my mind whispered back.

Tears welled behind my eyelids. No, it wasn't the trip. It was the fact I went out of my way to watch Tils's children whenever she needed a night out. I made Opece big meals and helped her with chores so she wouldn't get overwhelmed. And I remembered to get Drear's favorite tea when I was out trading because I knew her sister snuck into her stash.

I put forth so much effort and receive hardly any back.

Pulling up the blanket, I rolled over and tried to fall asleep. Lamenting wouldn't change anything. I tossed and turned, unable to relax until Huck finally came to bed and drew me close.

When dawn broke the next morning, the intensity of my emotions had faded, but I felt no less miserable. I grabbed my bag, gave Huck a goodbye kiss, and headed out.

The ricochet link I needed was stored with the others at the Traveler's Hollow.

My neighbors greeted me as I crossed the bridges. Their cheery mood and the crisp air lifted my spirits.

This is going to be a good day, I told myself.

The Traveler's Hollow held shelves of short wooden dowels stored in protective leather sleeves. Enchanted ricochet links were able to transport people between two points. The other halves of the link pairs were all over the world, letting us travel as we pleased.

An elf with deep red coloring shuffled out from behind the center column. "And where will you be going, Miss Venlo?"

I bowed my head in greeting. "It's time for my annual adventure, Ulix."

The old elf smiled and extended his hand. A smooth wooden dowel peeked out of the leather wrapping. To keep track of all the locations, dowels were stamped with an indicator on the end. This one had a yullis blossom on it.

I laughed. "You already knew."

"Well, the yullis season wouldn't be complete without the elf who started it all," Unlix replied. A hint of mischief twinkled in his eyes.

I reached out a finger, ready to press it against the wood, but guilt paused my hand. I looked over my shoulder. Tils wasn't in the hollow or on any of the pathways leading up to it.

My face hardened. I squashed the guilt. This was my trip. My one thing. I wasn't going to wait for her, and I was done trying to appease everyone instead of enjoying this sliver of happiness.

The moment my finger tapped the end of the dowel, my gut twisted. All the air whooshed out of my lungs, and pinpricks stung my skin. The Traveler's Hollow disappeared, and bright, bright sunlight consumed everything.

I gasped and raised my hand to guard my eyes. It took a while for my sight to adjust to a landscape without thick foliage.

Eventually, a cave made of tan rock came into focus. The second half of the dowel lay on the ground. This one, though, did not have a cover and was more worn due to exposure to the elements. Dust billowed around my bare feet as I walked outside.

The Ravines were a harsh land. Chunks of large rocks covered the earth, so very little could take root. The sun beat down and dried out any rain and moisture.

But giant mushrooms pushed through the tough landscape and climbed high into the sky regardless of the conditions. Some caps were curved, some were flat, and all were covered in plants. Vines swung in the light breeze, mimicking willow trees. Moss, flowers, and ferns adjusted to retain water and thrived on the caps.

When the largest mushrooms grew too close to the sun, they lost all their color and turned into stone. Sometimes the dwarrow used the petrified material to make weapons or jewelry, but not many people passed through here.

I adjusted my pack and started walking. Sharp stones scraped my feet, but such was the cost of traveling here. Shoes were a hindrance to my balance.

Yullis flowers liked flat caps on the tallest mushrooms so they could soak up as much sun as possible. In my first century, Huck helped me carve out a staircase in the stem of the largest one we could find.

The journey wasn't far, but I'd soon downed half a water skin and nibbled on a roll. Pregnancy was a new development, and I didn't quite know how my energy would be affected by my exertion.

I reached our yullis mushroom near midday and began climbing the corkscrew stairs. My eyes felt more sheltered, and although the enclosed space was stuffy, it was cooler than outside.

My toe caught on the edge of a step. Pitching forward, I cried out and landed hard on my knee. My voice echoed. Panting, I tugged off my pack and slipped down to lean against the wall.

"I guess it's time for a break," I told my belly. Chuckling to myself, I pulled out more water and took a sip. My knee was sore, but no real damage was done.

Despite the botched plans, blazing sun, and blistering weather, I was enjoying myself. My legs ached in a good way and my mind had quieted. A sense of peace settled over me. Once I'd caught my breath and quenched my dry throat, I continued.

When I was little, I used to mimic bird songs to see how many I could get to nest in the tree of our family hollow. My parents disliked the game at the discovery of the droppings. I'd since grown out of the childish habit, but the memory still replayed.

I pinched my lips together and whistled. The sharp tone bounced off the walls and filled my ears. I laughed at how off-key it was and tried another tune. There were no birds here, but I was free to make a fool of myself without an audience.

It seemed that in no time at all, I ascended the last few steps and popped out on the top of a large, flat mushroom cap.

My chin wobbled.

I usually came early in the season when the yullis patch was flush with flowers. Tangles of stringy vines matted down a bedding they liked to grow in.

The bright green was now a muted, dusty gray. All the yullis flowers were gone save three dried out husks.

I dropped my pack and sat, too overwhelmed with despair to continue looking at my once-beautiful patch. The sun didn't do damage to the vines; the many footprints stamping over them did. And the flowers left over were for the elves to feel good about "leaving some for the rest of us."

I took out my water skin and dribbled water on the wilted blossoms. They likely wouldn't survive, but I still wasn't going to pick them.

I swallowed the lump in my throat and went to head back when a flash of purple caught my eye. Curious, I crept towards the edge of the cap.

In the years since Huck and I searched, another massive mushroom had grown in the shadow of the one I stood on. Its dark orange cap had a small bump in the center, but it was flat enough the untouched yullis patch on it thrived.

I bit my lip.

The original patch I'd found had always been enough, but maybe it was time to find another. A patch I could nurture and protect. This one was too close; I'd have to search for a different spot.

Perhaps in the coming years I could pursue the idea. For now, I wanted to find a way onto the neighboring mushroom to gather a few flowers. It was too far down to jump comfortably. Elves were naturally good climbers, but climbing up from the ground wasn't an option either. The outside of the stem didn't have good holds, and even if I did make it up, I wasn't going to risk free-hanging the gills with a little one in my belly.

A gentle breeze drifted through the vines hanging off the caps.

A wild thought took root in my mind. I grinned. Tightening the straps on my sack, I crouched and mapped out my route. Some of the vines twisted together, and some dangled by themselves. I heaved up the biggest clump of vines I could comfortably grasp.

And jumped.

Wind whipped at my ears, stray leaves tickled my face, and the sun blinded my eyes.

I cackled with delight.

The orange cap rushed up, and I let go. Careful to roll on my shoulder to protect my midriff, I tumbled to a stop on my back.

My chest heaved, but it was the lightest it'd been in a long, long while.

"Oh, no!" I rushed out and scrambled to my feet. My landing crushed the yullis flowers in my path. I pulled out my second water skin and gave them a healthy pour.

Looking up, I realized the vines were a little higher from down here than I had originally thought, but I should still be able to grab them if I had a good running start. If all went well, I'd make it back to the ricochet link by dark and catch Huck for dinner.

I smiled and tugged out the empty bag from my sack. Whistling to myself, I gently picked every third flower until the bag was full. Yellow pollen from the stigmas coated my fingers, but I didn't mind.

Happiness burrowed its way into my heart. I felt calm here. Away from the buzz. Away from responsibility. Somewhere I could find peace in solitude.

I packed the flowers away and stood to leave. Looking one last time over the horizon, I rubbed my belly.

"Someday I'll take you here," I promised my little. "And someday I'll help you find your own haven."

Want more? Sign up to Arquie's newsletter for *Drizzle*, an exclusive standalone cozy fantasy short story!

Arquie *R-Q-E*
Noop *N-EW-P*
Krim *K-RIM*
Melki *MEL-KEY*
Farin *FAIR-IN*
Wynvi *WIN-VEE*
Pellin *P-EL-IN*
Venlo *VEN-LOW*

Denuce *D-EH-NOOSE* – *Type of blue mushroom. Very rare.*
Dima *DYE-MA* – *Small metal sigil used in the packs.*
Diopside *DYE-OP-SIDE* – *Type of green crystal.*
Dwarrow *D-WAR-OH* – *Plural of dwarf.*
Rizar *REE-ZAR* – *One of the wolf shifter packs.*
Rog *R-AW-G* – *Horned beast.*
Yullis *YOU-LIS* – *Type of rare flower.*

ACKNOWLEDGEMENTS

What started off as a silly little project hit home a little harder than I thought it would. A big shoutout to my husband, who supported me day after day, on the ups and downs, and everything in between. I'm also fortunate to have a circle of family and friends who've cheered me on every step of the way. My editor, Clara, and my early readers have helped me hone my skills as a writer and I've very grateful for all their feedback.

I wouldn't be nearly as far along in my writing career without my writing group. From sprints to deep conversations, the writers I've connected with have pushed me to keep going.

Of Becoming was inspired (very loosely) by experiences during my younger adult years. Some friends have stuck with me through it all, some I've lost, and some have been made along the way. Growing up is hard. Being out on your own is hard. You're not alone, and I hope my stories shared a bit of comfort.

Arquie spent her younger years staying up way too late reading books. Let's be honest, that hasn't changed much. She enjoys fantasy novels packed full of adventure and mayhem.

Arquie takes inspiration from her childhood growing up in eastern Montana, too many nature documentaries to count, and discovering niche interests. She looks up to creatives like Christopher Paolini, Kathryn Lasky, James Cameron, and Tatiana Maslany.

Now, she's bringing her own stories to life. You can find her curled up with a good book, hyper fixating on a new hobby, or writing her next adventure.